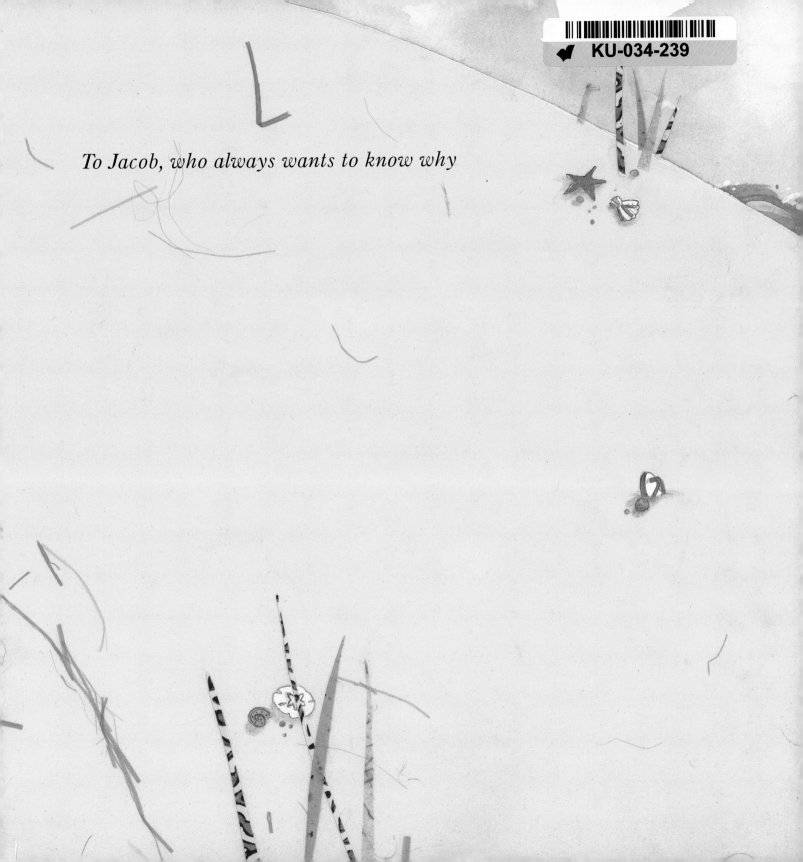

*To Jacob, who always wants to know why*

Stella and Sam were spending a day at the beach.
It was Sam's very first time.

# STELLA

## STAR OF THE SEA

### MARIE-LOUISE GAY

ALLEN & UNWIN

Published in the UK in 1999
by Allen & Unwin Ltd
19 Compton Terrace
London N1 2UN
Phone: (44 171) 704 0033
Fax: (44 171) 704 2266
E-mail: Allanunwin@compuserve.com

Published in Australia in 1999
by Allen & Unwin
9 Atchison Street
St Leonards NSW 1590
Australia
Phone: (61 2) 8425 0100
Fax: (61 2) 9906 2218
E-mail: frontdesk@allen-unwin.com.au
Web: http://www.allen-unwin.com.au

National Library of Australia
Cataloguing-in-Publication entry:

Gay, Marie-Louise.
Stella, star of the sea.

ISBN 1 86508 174 4 (pbk.).

I. Title.

813.54

First published in Canada in 1999
by Groundwood Books Limited

Printed in China by Everbest Printing Co. Ltd.

3 5 7 9 10 8 6 4 2

"Isn't it beautiful, Sam?" asked Stella.
"It's very big," said Sam, "and noisy."

Stella had seen the sea once, before Sam was born.
She knew all its secrets.

"Is the water cold?" asked Sam. "Is it deep?
Are there any sea monsters?"

"The water is lovely," said Stella.
"And not a sea monster in sight.
Come on in, Sam!"

"Not right now," said Sam.

"Where do starfish come from?" asked Sam.
"From the sky," answered Stella.

"Starfish are shooting stars
that fell in love with the sea."

"Weren't the stars afraid of drowning?" asked Sam.

"No," said Stella. "They all learned how to swim."

"What is this?" asked Sam.
"It's a moon shell," said Stella. "It comes from the moon."
"What is that?" asked Sam.

"It's an angel wing," said Stella. "It comes from an angel."
"And this?" asked Sam.
"It's a shark's eye," said Stella.

"Do you think there are sharks in the sea?" asked Sam.
"Have you ever seen one?"

"Just a little one," said Stella, "with an eyepatch.
Are you coming, Sam?"
"Not just this minute," said Sam.

"Come see, Sam," called Stella. "I found a sea horse."

"Does a sea horse neigh?" asked Sam.
"Does a sea horse gallop?"

"Yes!" cried Stella. "And you can ride a sea horse bareback. Come on in, Sam!"

"Not right now," said Sam.

"Let's dig a very deep hole," said Stella.

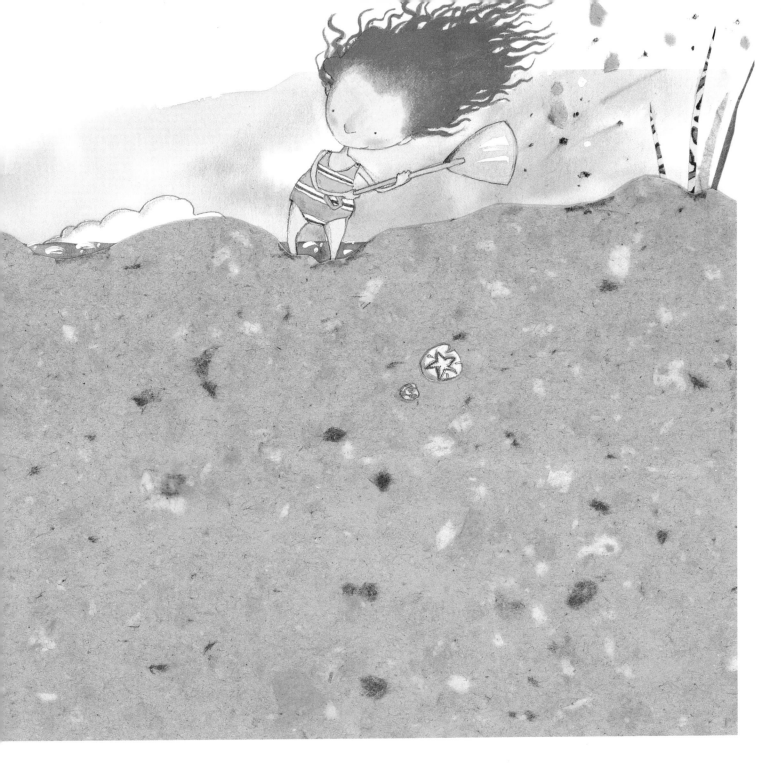

"Why?" asked Sam. "What for?
Where will we end up?"

"In China," answered Stella.
"Are we there yet?" asked Sam.

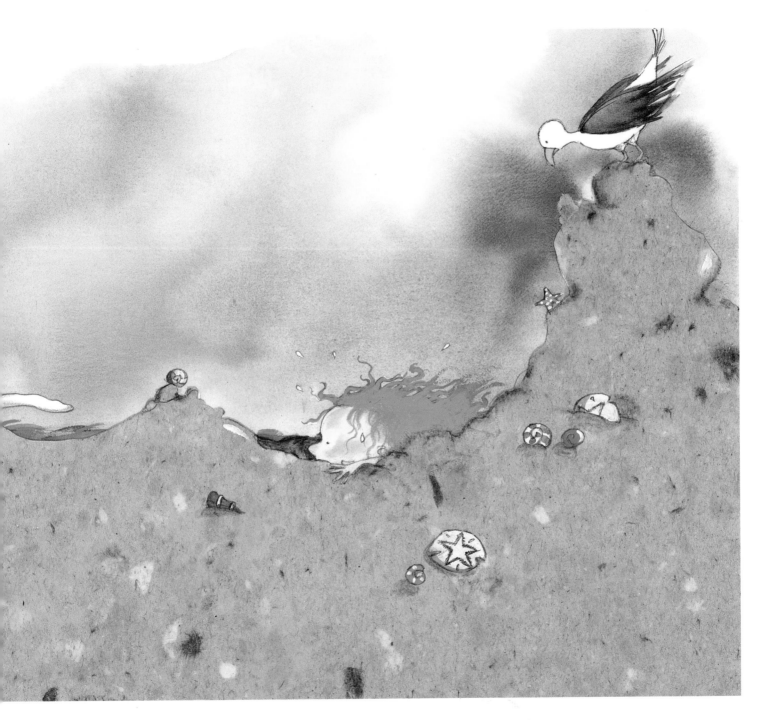

"Let's go fishing, Sam," sighed Stella.
"Maybe we'll catch a catfish."

"Does a catfish purr?" asked Sam.
"Does a dogfish bark?
Does a toadfish croak?" asked Sam.

"I don't know," sighed Stella. "I'm going swimming."
"Does a parrotfish swim?" asked Sam.
"Or does it fly and squawk?"

"Does the sea touch the sky?" asked Sam.
"Do boats sail off the edge?
Where do waves come from? Why..."

"Sam!!" yelled Stella. "Are you ever coming in?"

"YES!" said Sam.